WHAT
DADDIES
DO BEST

SIMON & SCHUSTER BOOKS FOR YOUNG READERS
New York London Toronto Sydney Singapore

WHAT DADDIES DO BEST

BY Laura Numeroff

ILLUSTRATED BY Lynn Munsinger

Daddies can teach you
how to ride a bicycle,

make a snowman with you,

and bake a delicious
cake for your birthday.

Daddies can help you
make a garden grow,

give you a
piggyback ride,

and take care of you
when you're sick.

Daddies can watch
the sun set with you,

sew the loose button
on your teddy bear,

and hold you when
you're feeling sad.

Daddies can take you
trick-or-treating,

help you give the
dog a bath,

and play with you
in the park.

Daddies can read you
a bedtime story,

tuck you in,

and kiss you good-night.

But best of all,
daddies can give you
lots and lots of love!